The Yellow
Wallpaper

The Yellow Wallpaper

Charlotte Perkins Gilman

Afterword by Elaine R. Hedges

The Feminist Press
at The City University of New York

Manufactured in the United States of America.

First edition, seventeenth printing

Library of Congress Cataloging in Publication Data
Gilman, Charlotte (Perkins) Stetson, 1860-1935.
The yellow wallpaper.
(Feminist Press reprint series)
Reprint of the 1899 ed. published by Small, Maynard,
Boston.
Includes bibliographical references.
I. Title.
PZ3.G4204Ye6 [PS1744.G57]   813'.4   73-5795
ISBN 0-912670-09-6

Distributed by The Talman Company, Inc., 150 Fifth Avenue,
New York, N.Y. 10011.

Contents

The Yellow Wallpaper

It is very seldom that mere ordinary people like
John and myself secure ancestral halls for the sum-
mer.

A colonial mansion, a hereditary estate, I would
say a haunted house, and reach the height of
romantic felicity—but that would be asking too
much of fate!

Still I will proudly declare that there is something queer about it.

Else, why should it be let so cheaply? And why
have stood so long untenanted?

John laughs at me, of course, but one expects
that in marriage.

John is practical in the extreme. He has no
patience with faith, an intense horror of supersti-
tion, and he scoffs openly at any talk of things
not to be felt and seen and put down in figures.

John is a physician, and *perhaps*—(I would not

say it to a living soul, of course, but this is dead paper and a great relief to my mind)— *perhaps* that is one reason I do not get well faster.

You see he does not believe I am sick!

And what can one do?

If a physician of high standing, and one's own husband, assures friends and relatives that there is really nothing the matter with one but temporary nervous depression—a slight hysterical tendency— what is one to do?

My brother is also a physician, and also of high standing, and he says the same thing.

So I take phosphates or phospites—whichever it is, and tonics, and journeys, and air, and exercise, and am absolutely forbidden to "work" until I am well again.

Personally, I disagree with their ideas.

Personally, I believe that congenial work, with excitement and change, would do me good.

But what is one to do?

I did write for a while in spite of them; but it *does* exhaust me a good deal—having to be so sly about it, or else meet with heavy opposition.

I sometimes fancy that in my condition if I had less opposition and more society and stimulus—but John says the very worst thing I can do is to think about my condition, and I confess it always makes me feel bad.

So I will let it alone and talk about the house.

The most beautiful place! It is quite alone, standing well back from the road, quite three miles from the village. It makes me think of English places that you read about, for there are hedges and walls and gates that lock, and lots of separate little houses for the gardeners and people.

There is a *delicious* garden! I never saw such a garden—large and shady, full of box-bordered paths, and lined with long grape-covered arbors with seats under them.

There were greenhouses, too, but they are all broken now.

There was some legal trouble, I believe, something about the heirs and coheirs; anyhow, the place has been empty for years.

That spoils my ghostliness, I am afraid, but I don't care—there is something strange about the house—I can feel it.

I even said so to John one moonlight evening, but he said what I felt was a *draught,* and shut the window.

I get unreasonably angry with John sometimes. I'm sure I never used to be so sensitive. I think it is due to this nervous condition.

But John says if I feel so, I shall neglect proper self-control; so I take pains to control myself—before him, at least, and that makes me very tired.

I don't like our room a bit. I wanted one downstairs that opened on the piazza and had roses all over the window, and such pretty old-fashioned chintz hangings! but John would not hear of it.

He said there was only one window and not room for two beds, and no near room for him if he took another.

He is very careful and loving, and hardly lets me stir without special direction.

I have a schedule prescription for each hour in the day; he takes all care from me, and so I feel basely ungrateful not to value it more.

He said we came here solely on my account, that I was to have perfect rest and all the air I could get. "Your exercise depends on your strength, my dear," said he, "and your food somewhat on your appetite; but air you can absorb all the time." So we took the nursery at the top of the house.

It is a big, airy room, the whole floor nearly, with windows that look all ways, and air and sunshine galore. It was nursery first and then playroom and gymnasium, I should judge; for the windows are barred for little children, and there are rings and things in the walls.

The paint and paper look as if a boys' school had used it. It is stripped off—the paper—in great patches all around the head of my bed, about as far as I can reach, and in a great place on the other side of the room low down. I never saw a worse paper in my life.

One of those sprawling flamboyant patterns committing every artistic sin.

It is dull enough to confuse the eye in following, pronounced enough to constantly irritate and provoke study, and when you follow the lame uncertain curves for a little distance they suddenly commit suicide—plunge off at outrageous angles, destroy themselves in unheard of contradictions.

The color is repellent, almost revolting; a smouldering unclean yellow, strangely faded by the slow-turning sunlight.

It is a dull yet lurid orange in some places, a sickly sulphur tint in others.

No wonder the children hated it! I should hate it myself if I had to live in this room long.

There comes John, and I must put this away,— he hates to have me write a word.

We have been here two weeks, and I haven't felt like writing before, since that first day.

I am sitting by the window now, up in this atrocious nursery, and there is nothing to hinder my writing as much as I please, save lack of strength.

John is away all day, and even some nights when his cases are serious.

I am glad my case is not serious!

But these nervous troubles are dreadfully depressing.

John does not know how much I really suffer. He knows there is no *reason* to suffer, and that satisfies him.

Of course it is only nervousness. It does weigh on me so not to do my duty in any way!

I meant to be such a help to John, such a real rest and comfort, and here I am a comparative burden already!

Nobody would believe what an effort it is to do what little I am able,—to dress and entertain, and order things.

It is fortunate Mary is so good with the baby. Such a dear baby!

And yet I *cannot* be with him, it makes me so nervous.

I suppose John never was nervous in his life. He laughs at me so about this wall-paper!

At first he meant to repaper the room, but afterwards he said that I was letting it get the better of me, and that nothing was worse for a nervous patient than to give way to such fancies.

He said that after the wall-paper was changed it would be the heavy bedstead, and then the barred windows, and then that gate at the head of the stairs, and so on.

"You know the place is doing you good," he said, "and really, dear, I don't care to renovate the house just for a three months' rental."

"Then do let us go downstairs," I said, "there are such pretty rooms there."

Then he took me in his arms and called me a blessed little goose, and said he would go down to the cellar, if I wished, and have it whitewashed into the bargain.

But he is right enough about the beds and windows and things.

It is an airy and comfortable room as any one need wish, and, of course, I would not be so silly as to make him uncomfortable just for a whim.

I'm really getting quite fond of the big room, all but that horrid paper.

Out of one window I can see the garden, those mysterious deepshaded arbors, the riotous old-fashioned flowers, and bushes and gnarly trees.

Out of another I get a lovely view of the bay and a little private wharf belonging to the estate. There is a beautiful shaded lane that runs down there from the house. I always fancy I see people walking in these numerous paths and arbors, but John has cautioned me not to give way to fancy in the least. He says that with my imaginative power and habit of story-making, a nervous weakness like mine is sure to lead to all manner of excited fancies, and that I ought to use my will and good sense to check the tendency. So I try.

I think sometimes that if I were <u>only well enough to write a little it would relieve the press of ideas</u> and rest me.

But I find I get pretty tired when I try.

It is <u>so discouraging not to have any advice and companionship about my work</u>. When I get really well, John says we will ask Cousin Henry and Julia down for a long visit; but he says he would as soon put fireworks in my pillow-case as to let me have <u>those stimulating people about</u> now.

I wish I could get well faster.

But I must not think about that. This paper looks to me as if it *knew* what a vicious influence it had!

There is a recurrent spot where the pattern lolls like a broken neck and two bulbous eyes stare at you upside down.

I get positively angry with the impertinence of it and the everlastingness. Up and down and sideways they crawl, and those absurd, unblinking eyes are everywhere. There is one place where two breaths didn't match, and the eyes go all up and down the line, one a little higher than the other.

I never saw so much expression in an inanimate thing before, and we all know how much expression they have! I used to lie awake as a child and get more entertainment and terror out of blank walls and plain furniture than most children could find in a toy-store.

I remember what a kindly wink the knobs of our big, old bureau used to have, and there was one chair that always seemed like a strong friend.

I used to feel that if any of the other things looked too fierce I could always hop into that chair and be safe.

The furniture in this room is no worse than inharmonious, however, for we had to bring it all from downstairs. I suppose when this was used as a playroom they had to take the nursery things out, and no wonder! I never saw such ravages as the children have made here.

The wall-paper, as I said before, is torn off in spots, and it sticketh closer than a brother—they must have had perseverance as well as hatred.

Then the floor is scratched and gouged and splintered, the plaster itself is dug out here and there, and this great heavy bed which is all we found in the room, looks as if it had been through the wars.

But I don't mind it a bit—only the paper.

There comes John's sister. Such a dear girl as she is, and so careful of me! I must not let her find me writing.

She is a perfect and enthusiastic housekeeper,

and hopes for no better profession. I verily believe she thinks it is the writing which made me sick!

But I can write when she is out, and see her a long way off from these windows.

There is one that commands the road, a lovely shaded winding road, and one that just looks off over the country. A lovely country, too, full of great elms and velvet meadows.

This wall-paper has a kind of sub-pattern in a different shade, a particularly irritating one, for you can only see it in certain lights, and not clearly then.

But in the places where it isn't faded and where the sun is just so—I can see a strange, provoking, formless sort of figure, that seems to skulk about behind that silly and conspicuous front design.

There's sister on the stairs!

Well, the Fourth of July is over! The people are all gone and I am tired out. John thought it might do me good to see a little company, so we just had mother and Nellie and the children down for a week.

Of course I didn't do a thing. Jennie sees to everything now.

But it tired me all the same.

John says if I don't pick up faster he shall send me to Weir Mitchell in the fall.

But I don't want to go there at all. I had a friend who was in his hands once, and she says he is just like John and my brother, only more so!

Besides, it is such an undertaking to go so far.

I don't feel as if it was worth while to turn my hand over for anything, and I'm getting dreadfully fretful and querulous.

I cry at nothing, and cry most of the time.

Of course I don't when John is here, or anybody else, but when I am alone.

And I am alone a good deal just now. John is kept in town very often by serious cases, and Jennie is good and lets me alone when I want her to.

So I walk a little in the garden or down that lovely lane, sit on the porch under the roses, and lie down up here a good deal.

I'm getting really fond of the room in spite of the wall-paper. Perhaps *because* of the wall-paper.

It dwells in my mind so!

I lie here on this great immovable bed—it is nailed down, I believe—and follow that pattern about by the hour. It is as good as gymnastics, I assure you. I start, we'll say, at the bottom, down in the corner over there where it has not been touched, and I determine for the thousandth time that I *will* follow that pointless pattern to some sort of a conclusion.

I know a little of the principle of design, and I know this thing was not arranged on any laws of radiation, or alternation, or repetition, or symmetry, or anything else that I ever heard of.

It is repeated, of course, by the breadths, but not otherwise.

Looked at in one way each breadth stands alone, the bloated curves and flourishes—a kind of "debased Romanesque" with *delirium tremens*—go waddling up and down in isolated columns of fatuity.

But, on the other hand, they connect diagonally, and the sprawling outlines run off in great slanting waves of optic horror, like a lot of wallowing seaweeds in full chase.

The whole thing goes horizontally, too, at least it seems so, and I exhaust myself in trying to distinguish the order of its going in that direction.

They have used a horizontal breadth for a frieze, and that adds wonderfully to the confusion.

There is one end of the room where it is almost intact, and there, when the crosslights fade and the low sun shines directly upon it, I can almost fancy radiation after all,—the interminable grotesques seem to form around a common centre and rush off in headlong plunges of equal distraction.

It makes me tired to follow it. I will take a nap I guess.

I don't know why I should write this.

I don't want to.

I don't feel able.

And I know John would think it absurd. But I *must* say what I feel and think in some way—it is such a relief!

But the effort is getting to be greater than the relief.

Half the time now I am awfully lazy, and lie down ever so much.

John says I mustn't lose my strength, and has me take cod liver oil and lots of tonics and things, to say nothing of ale and wine and rare meat.

Dear John! He loves me very dearly, and hates to have me sick. I tried to have a real earnest reasonable talk with him the other day, and tell him how I wish he would let me go and make a visit to Cousin Henry and Julia.

But he said I wasn't able to go, nor able to stand it after I got there; and I did not make out a very good case for myself, for I was crying before I had finished.

It is getting to be a great effort for me to think straight. Just this nervous weakness I suppose.

And dear John gathered me up in his arms, and just carried me upstairs and laid me on the bed, and sat by me and read to me till it tired my head.

He said I was his darling and his comfort and all

he had, and that I must take care of myself for his sake, and keep well.

He says no one but myself can help me out of it, that I must use my will and self-control and not let any silly fancies run away with me.

There's one comfort, the baby is well and happy, and does not have to occupy this nursery with the horrid wall-paper.

If we had not used it, that blessed child would have! What a fortunate escape! Why, I wouldn't have a child of mine, an impressionable little thing, live in such a room for worlds.

I never thought of it before, but it is lucky that John kept me here after all, I can stand it so much easier than a baby, you see.

Of course I never mention it to them any more—I am too wise,—but I keep watch of it all the same.

There are things in that paper that nobody knows but me, or ever will.

Behind that outside pattern the dim shapes get clearer every day.

It is always the same shape, only very numerous.

And it is like a woman stooping down and creeping about behind that pattern. I don't like it a bit. I wonder—I begin to think—I wish John would take me away from here!

Charlotte Perkins Gilman 22

It is so hard to talk with John about my case, because he is so wise, and because he loves me so.

But I tried it last night.

It was moonlight. The moon shines in all around just as the sun does.

I hate to see it sometimes, it creeps so slowly, and always comes in by one window or another.

John was asleep and I hated to waken him, so I kept still and watched the moonlight on that undulating wall-paper till I felt creepy.

The faint figure behind seemed to shake the pattern, just as if she wanted to get out.

I got up softly and went to feel and see if the paper *did* move, and when I came back John was awake.

"What is it, little girl?" he said. "Don't go walking about like that—you'll get cold."

I thought it was a good time to talk, so I told him that I really was not gaining here, and that I wished he would take me away.

"Why darling!" said he, "our lease will be up in three weeks, and I can't see how to leave before.

"The repairs are not done at home, and I cannot possibly leave town just now. Of course if you were in any danger, I could and would, but you really are better, dear, whether you can see it or not. I am a doctor, dear, and I know. You are gaining flesh and color, your appetite is better, I feel really much easier about you."

"I don't weigh a bit more," said I, "nor as much; and my appetite may be better in the evening when you are here, but it is worse in the morning when you are away!"

"Bless her little heart!" said he with a big hug, "she shall be as sick as she pleases! But now let's improve the shining hours by going to sleep, and talk about it in the morning!"

"And you won't go away?" I asked gloomily.

"Why, how can I, dear? It is only three weeks more and then we will take a nice little trip of a few days while Jennie is getting the house ready. Really dear you are better!"

"Better in body perhaps——" I began, and stopped short, for he sat up straight and looked at me with such a stern, reproachful look that I could not say another word.

"My darling," said he, "I beg of you, for my sake and for our child's sake, as well as for your own, that you will never for one instant let that idea enter your mind! There is nothing so dangerous, so fascinating, to a temperament like yours. It is a false and foolish fancy. Can you not trust me as a physician when I tell you so?"

So of course I said no more on that score, and

we went to sleep before long. He thought I was asleep first, but I wasn't, and lay there for hours trying to decide whether that front pattern and the back pattern really did move together or separately.

On a pattern like this, by daylight, there is a lack of sequence, a defiance of law, that is a constant irritant to a normal mind.

The color is hideous enough, and unreliable enough, and infuriating enough, but the pattern is torturing.

You think you have mastered it, but just as you get well underway in following, it turns a back-somersault and there you are. It slaps you in the face, knocks you down, and tramples upon you. It is like a bad dream.

The outside pattern is a florid arabesque, reminding one of a fungus. If you can imagine a toadstool in joints, an interminable string of toadstools, budding and sprouting in endless convolutions—why, that is something like it.

That is, sometimes!

There is one marked peculiarity about this paper, a thing nobody seems to notice but myself, and that is that it changes as the light changes.

When the sun shoots in through the east window—I always watch for that first long, straight ray—it changes so quickly that I never can quite believe it.

That is why I watch it always.

By moonlight—the moon shines in all night when there is a moon—I wouldn't know it was the same paper.

At night in any kind of light, in twilight, candle light, lamplight, and worst of all by moonlight, it becomes bars! The outside pattern I mean, and the woman behind it is as plain as can be.

I didn't realize for a long time what the thing was that showed behind, that dim sub-pattern, but now I am quite sure it is a woman.

By daylight she is subdued, quiet. I fancy it is the pattern that keeps her so still. It is so puzzling. It keeps me quiet by the hour.

I lie down ever so much now. John says it is good for me, and to sleep all I can.

Indeed he started the habit by making me lie down for an hour after each meal.

It is a very bad habit I am convinced, for you see I don't sleep.

And that cultivates deceit, for I don't tell them I'm awake—O no!

The fact is I am getting a little afraid of John.

He seems very queer sometimes, and even Jennie has an inexplicable look.

It strikes me occasionally, just as a scientific hypothesis,—that perhaps it is the paper!

I have watched John when he did not know I was looking, and come into the room suddenly on the most innocent excuses, and I've caught him several times *looking at the paper!* And Jennie too. I caught Jennie with her hand on it once.

She didn't know I was in the room, and when I asked her in a quiet, a very quiet voice, with the most restrained manner possible, what she was doing with the paper—she turned around as if she had been caught stealing, and looked quite angry— asked me why I should frighten her so!

Then she said that the paper stained everything it touched, that she had found yellow smooches on all my clothes and John's, and she wished we would be more careful!

Did not that sound innocent? But I know she was studying that pattern, and I am determined that nobody shall find it out but myself!

Life is very much more exciting now than it used to be. You see I have something more to expect, to look forward to, to watch. I really do eat better, and am more quiet than I was.

John is so pleased to see me improve! He laughed a little the other day, and said I seemed to be flourishing in spite of my wall-paper.

I turned it off with a laugh. I had no intention of telling him it was *because* of the wall-paper—he would make fun of me. He might even want to take me away.

I don't want to leave now until I have found it out. There is a week more, and I think that will be enough.

I'm feeling ever so much better! I don't sleep much at night, for it is so interesting to watch developments; but I sleep a good deal in the day-time.

In the daytime it is tiresome and perplexing.

There are always new shoots on the fungus, and new shades of yellow all over it. I cannot keep count of them, though I have tried conscientiously.

It is the strangest yellow, that wall-paper! It makes me think of all the yellow things I ever saw—not beautiful ones like buttercups, but old foul, bad yellow things.

But there is something else about that paper— the smell! I noticed it the moment we came into the room, but with so much air and sun it was not bad. Now we have had a week of fog and rain, and whether the windows are open or not, the smell is here.

It creeps all over the house.

I find it hovering in the dining-room, skulking in

the parlor, hiding in the hall, lying in wait for me on the stairs.

It gets into my hair.

Even when I go to ride, if I turn my head suddenly and surprise it—there is that smell!

Such a peculiar odor, too! I have spent hours in trying to analyze it, to find what it smelled like.

It is not bad—at first, and very gentle, but quite the subtlest, most enduring odor I ever met.

In this damp weather it is awful, I wake up in the night and find it hanging over me.

It used to disturb me at first. I thought seriously of burning the house—to reach the smell.

But now I am used to it. The only thing I can think of that it is like is the *color* of the paper! A yellow smell.

There is a very funny mark on this wall, low down, near the mopboard. A streak that runs round the room. It goes behind every piece of furniture, except the bed, a long, straight, even *smooch,* as if it had been rubbed over and over.

I wonder how it was done and who did it, and what they did it for. Round and round and round—round and round and round—it makes me dizzy!

I really have discovered something at last.

Through watching so much at night, when it

changes so, I have finally found out.

The front pattern *does* move— and no wonder! The woman behind shakes it!

Sometimes I think there are a great many women behind, and sometimes only one, and she crawls around fast, and her crawling shakes it all over.

Then in the very bright spots she keeps still, and in the very shady spots she just takes hold of the bars and shakes them hard.

And she is all the time trying to climb through. But nobody could climb through that pattern—it strangles so; I think that is why it has so many heads.

They get through, and then the pattern strangles them off and turns them upside down, and makes their eyes white!

If those heads were covered or taken off it would not be half so bad.

I think that woman gets out in the daytime!

And I'll tell you why—privately—I've seen her!

I can see her out of every one of my windows!

It is the same woman, I know, for she is always creeping, and most women do not creep by daylight.

I see her on that long road under the trees, creeping along, and when a carriage comes she hides under the blackberry vines.

I don't blame her a bit. It must be very humiliating to be caught creeping by daylight!

I always lock the door when I creep by daylight. I can't do it at night, for I know John would suspect something at once.

And John is so queer now, that I don't want to irritate him. I wish he would take another room! Besides, I don't want anybody to get that woman out at night but myself.

I often wonder if I could see her out of all the windows at once.

But, turn as fast as I can, I can only see out of one at one time.

And though I always see her, she *may* be able to creep faster than I can turn!

I have watched her sometimes away off in the open country, creeping as fast as a cloud shadow in a high wind.

If only that top pattern could be gotten off from the under one! I mean to try it, little by little.

I have found out another funny thing, but I shan't tell it this time! It does not do to trust people too much.

There are only two more days to get this paper off, and I believe John is beginning to notice. I don't like the look in his eyes.

And I heard him ask Jennie a lot of professional questions about me. She had a very good report to give.

She said I slept a good deal in the daytime.

John knows I don't sleep very well at night, for all I'm so quiet!

He asked me all sorts of questions, too, and pretended to be very loving and kind.

As if I couldn't see through him!

Still, I don't wonder he acts so, sleeping under this paper for three months.

It only interests me, but I feel sure John and Jennie are secretly affected by it.

Hurrah! This is the last day, but it is enough. John to stay in town over night, and won't be out until this evening.

Jennie wanted to sleep with me—the sly thing! but I told her I should undoubtedly rest better for a night all alone.

That was clever, for really I wasn't alone a bit! As soon as it was moonlight and that poor thing began to crawl and shake the pattern, I got up and ran to help her.

I pulled and she shook, I shook and she pulled, and before morning we had peeled off yards of that paper.

A strip about as high as my head and half around the room.

And then when the sun came and that awful pattern began to laugh at me, I declared I would finish it to-day!

We go away to-morrow, and they are moving all my furniture down again to leave things as they were before.

Jennie looked at the wall in amazement, but I told her merrily that I did it out of pure spite at the vicious thing.

She laughed and said she wouldn't mind doing it herself, but I must not get tired.

How she betrayed herself that time!

But I am here, and no person touches this paper but me,—not *alive!*

She tried to get me out of the room—it was too patent! But I said it was so quiet and empty and clean now that I believed I would lie down again and sleep all I could; and not to wake me even for dinner—I would call when I woke.

So now she is gone, and the servants are gone, and the things are gone, and there is nothing left but that great bedstead nailed down, with the canvas mattress we found on it.

We shall sleep downstairs to-night, and take the boat home to-morrow.

I quite enjoy the room, now it is bare again.

How those children did tear about here!

This bedstead is fairly gnawed!

But I must get to work.

I have locked the door and thrown the key down into the front path.

I don't want to go out, and I don't want to have anybody come in, till John comes.

I want to astonish him.

I've got a rope up here that even Jennie did not find. If that woman does get out, and tries to get away, I can tie her!

But I forgot I could not reach far without anything to stand on!

This bed will *not* move!

I tried to lift and push it until I was lame, and then I got so angry I bit off a little piece at one corner—but it hurt my teeth.

Then I peeled off all the paper I could reach standing on the floor. It sticks horribly and the pattern just enjoys it! All those strangled heads and bulbous eyes and waddling fungus growths just shriek with derision!

I am getting angry enough to do something desperate. To jump out of the window would be admirable exercise, but the bars are too strong even to try.

Besides I wouldn't do it. Of course not. I know

well enough that a step like that is improper and might be misconstrued.

I don't like to *look* out of the windows even—there are so many of those creeping women, and they creep so fast.

I wonder if they all come out of that wall-paper as I did?

But I am securely fastened now by my well-hidden rope—you don't get *me* out in the road there!

I suppose I shall have to get back behind the pattern when it comes night, and that is hard!

It is so pleasant to be out in this great room and creep around as I please!

I don't want to go outside. I won't, even if Jennie asks me to.

For outside you have to creep on the ground, and everything is green instead of yellow.

But here I can creep smoothly on the floor, and my shoulder just fits in that long smooch around the wall, so I cannot lose my way.

Why there's John at the door!

It is no use, young man, you can't open it!

How he does call and pound!

Now he's crying for an axe.

It would be a shame to break down that beautiful door!

"John dear!" said I in the gentlest voice, "the key is down by the front steps, under a plantain leaf!"

That silenced him for a few moments.

Then he said—very quietly indeed, "Open the door, my darling!"

"I can't," said I. "The key is down by the front door under a plantain leaf!"

And then I said it again, several times, very gently and slowly, and said it so often that he had to go and see, and he got it of course, and came in. He stopped short by the door.

"What is the matter?" he cried. "For God's sake, what are you doing!"

I kept on creeping just the same, but I looked at him over my shoulder.

"I've got out at last," said I, "in spite of you and Jane. And I've pulled off most of the paper, so you can't put me back!"

Now why should that man have fainted? But he did, and right across my path by the wall, so that I had to creep over him every time!

Afterword by Elaine R. Hedges

"The Yellow Wallpaper" is a small literary masterpiece. For almost fifty years it has been overlooked, as has its author, one of the most commanding feminists of her time. Now, with the new growth of the feminist movement, Charlotte Perkins Gilman is being rediscovered, and "The Yellow Wallpaper" should share in that rediscovery. The story of a woman's mental breakdown, narrated with superb psychological and dramatic precision, it is, as William Dean Howells said of it in 1920, a story to "freeze our . . . blood."[1]

The story was wrenched out of Gilman's own life, and is unique in the canon of her works. Although she wrote other fiction—short stories and novels—and much poetry as well, none of it ever achieved the power and directness, the imaginative authenticity of this piece. Polemical intent often made her fiction dry and clumsily didactic; and the extraordinary pressures of publishing deadlines under which she worked made careful composition almost impossible. (During one seven-year period she edited and published her own magazine, *The Forerunner*, writing almost all of the material for it—a sum total, she estimated, of twenty-one thousand words per month or the equivalent of twenty-eight books.)

Charlotte Perkins Gilman was an active feminist and primarily a nonfiction writer: the author of *Women and Economics*, a witty, bitingly satirical analysis of the situation of women in her society, which was used as a college text in the 1920s and translated into seven languages; and the author of many other nonfiction works dealing with the socioeconomic status of women. She was also an indefatigable and inspiring lecturer. Her work during the last decade of the nineteenth century and the first two of the twentieth has led one recent historian to say that she was "the leading intellectual in the women's movement in the United States" in her time.[2]

That interest in her has recently revived is satisfying, and only just. In the past few years several masters theses and doctoral dissertations have been written about her, and *Women and Economics* was reissued in 1966. The recent acquisition of her personal papers by the Schlesinger Library of Radcliffe College is bound to lead to further research and publication. Even "The Yellow Wallpaper" has resurfaced in several anthologies. However, tucked away among many other selections and frequently with only brief biographical information about its author, the story will not necessarily find in these anthologies the wide audience it deserves.[3]

Yet it does deserve the widest possible audience. For aside from the light it throws on the personal despairs, and the artistic triumph over them, of one of America's foremost feminists, the story is one of the rare pieces of literature we have by a nineteenth-century woman which directly confronts the sexual politics of the male-female, husband-wife relationship. In its time (and presumably still today, given its appearance in the anthology *Psychopathology and Literature*), the story was read essentially as a Poe-esque tale of chilling horror—and as a story of mental aberration. It is both of these. But it is more. It is a feminist document, dealing with sexual politics at a time when few writers felt free to do so, at least so candidly. Three years after Gilman published her story, Kate Chopin published *The Awakening*, a novel so frank in its treatment of the middle-class wife and her prescribed submissive role that it lost its author both reputation and income. It is symptomatic of their times that both Gilman's story and Chopin's novel end with the self-destruction of their heroines.

It wasn't easy for Charlotte Perkins Gilman to get her story published. She sent it first to William Dean Howells, and he, responding to at least some of its power and authenticity, recommended it to Horace Scudder, editor of *The Atlantic Monthly,* then the most prestigious magazine in the United States. Scudder rejected the story, according to Gilman's account in her autobiography, with a curt note:

Dear Madam,

Mr. Howells has handed me this story.
I could not forgive myself if I made others as miserable as I have made myself!

Sincerely yours,[4]
H.E. Scudder

In the 1890s editors, and especially Scudder, still officially adhered to a canon of "moral uplift" in literature, and Gilman's story, with its heroine reduced at the end to the level of a groveling animal, scarcely fitted the prescribed formula. One wonders, however, whether hints of the story's attack on social mores—specifically on the ideal of the submissive wife—came through to Scudder and unsettled him?

The story was finally published, in May 1892, in *The New England Magazine*, where it was greeted with strong but mixed feelings. Gilman was warned that such stories were "perilous stuff," which should not be printed because of the threat they posed to the relatives of such "deranged" persons as the heroine.[5] The implications of such warnings—that women should "stay in their place," that nothing could or should be done except maintain silence or conceal problems—are fairly clear. Those who praised the story, for the accuracy of its portrayal and its delicacy of touch, did so on the grounds that Gilman had captured in literature, from a medical point of view, the most "detailed account of incipient insanity."[6] Howells' admiration for the story, when he reprinted it in 1920 in the *Great Modern American Stories*, limited itself to the story's "chilling" quality. Again, however, no one seems to have made the connection between the insanity and the sex, or sexual role, of the victim, no one explored the story's implications for male-female relationships in the nineteenth century.

To appreciate fully these relationships, and hence the meaning of Gilman's story, requires biographical background. Born in 1860 in Connecticut, Charlotte Perkins grew up in Rhode Island and her childhood and youth were hard. Her mother bore three children in three years; one child died; after the birth of the third the father abandoned the family. Charlotte said of her mother that her life was "one of the most painfully thwarted I have ever known." Her mother had been idolized as a young girl, had had many suitors, and was then left with two children after a few brief years of marriage. Did the conflicting patterns imposed on women at that time (and still today)—"belle of the ball" versus housewife and producer of children—contribute to, or indeed even account for, the destruction of her marriage? Gilman suggests that the father may have left the family because the mother had been told that if she were to have another child she might die.[7] In any event, the effect of the broken marriage on Charlotte was painful. According to Gilman's autobiography, her mother sacrificed both her own and her daughter's need for love, out of an understandably desperate yet inevitably self-destructive need for protection against further betrayal; the mother seems literally to have refused so much as a light physical caress. It was her way of initiating Charlotte into the sufferings that life would hold for a woman.

Growing up without tenderness Charlotte grew up also, perhaps as a result of the treatment she received, determined to develop her willpower and refusing to be defeated. Her own description of herself at sixteen is of a person who had "My mother's profound religious tendency and implacable sense of duty; my father's intellectual appetite; a will power, well developed, from both; a passion of my own for scientific knowledge, for real laws of life; an insatiable demand for perfection in everything . . . ."[8] These traits would characterize her, and her work, throughout her life.

That, at seventeen, she could write, "Am going to try hard this winter to see if I cannot enjoy myself like other people" is both painful indication of the deprivations of her childhood and tribute to the strengths she wrested from those deprivations.[9] She had inherited the New England Puritan tradition of duty and responsibility: what she described as the development of "noble character."[10] (She was related to the famous Beecher family; Harriet Beecher Stowe was her great-aunt.) On the whole her Puritan heritage served her well; but it had its painful effects, as would be seen in her first marriage.

By the time she was in her late teens Charlotte Perkins had begun seriously to ponder "the injustices under which women suffered."[11] Although not in close touch with the suffrage movement (with which indeed she never in her later career directly associated herself, finding its objectives too limited for her own more radical views on the need for social change), she was becoming increasingly aware of such current developments as the entrance of some young women into colleges—and the ridicule they received—of the growing numbers of young women in the working population, of a few books being written that critically examined the institution of marriage, and of the somewhat more open discussion of matters of sexuality and chastity. She began to write poems—one in defense of prostitutes—and to pursue her own independent thinking. Her commitment was to change a world which she saw as unhappy and confused: she would use logic, argument, and demonstration; she would write and she would lecture.

Meanwhile she had met Charles Stetson, a Providence, Rhode Island, artist. She was drawn to him by his artistic ability, his ideals, and his loneliness—so much like her own. The story of their courtship, as she recounts it in her autobiography, is evidence of the effects on her of the life of self-denial she had led. There was, she says, "no natural response of inclination or desire, no question of, 'Do I love him?' only, 'Is it right?' " Only after reluctance and refusal, and at a time when he had met with "a keen personal disappointment," did she agree to marry him.[12] Actually, her motives in marrying, and her expectations of marriage are, until further evidence is available, difficult to sort out. Although her autobiography stresses her sense of duty and pity there seems also to be evidence, from some early notebooks and journals at the Schlesinger Library, that love and companionship were also involved. But what is clear is that Charlotte Perkins knew she was facing the crucial question so many nineteenth-century women had to face: marriage or a career. A woman "*should* be able to have marriage and motherhood, and do her work in the world also," she argued.[13] Yet she was not convinced by her own argument—what models did she have? And her fears that marriage and motherhood might incapacitate her for her "work in the world" would prove to be true, for her as for most women in our society.

Although she claims to have been happy with her husband, who was "tender" and "devoted," and helped with the housework, and toward whom she felt "the natural force of sex-attraction," she soon began to experience periods of depression: ". . . something was going wrong from the first." As she describes it, "A sort of gray fog drifted

across my mind, a cloud that grew and darkened."
Increasingly she felt weak, sleepless, unable to
work. A year after the marriage she gave birth to a
daughter and within a month of the birth she
became, again in her own words, "a mental
wreck." There was a constant dragging weari-
ness. . . . Absolute incapacity. Absolute misery." [14]

It would seem that Charlotte Perkins Stetson felt
trapped by the role assigned the wife within the
conventional nineteenth century marriage. If
marriage meant children and too many children
meant incapacity for other work; if she saw her
father's abandonment and her mother's coldness as
the result of this sexual-marital bind; if she saw
herself as victimized by marriage, the woman
playing the passive role—then she was simply seeing
clearly.

It was out of this set of marital circumstances,
but beyond that out of her larger social awareness
of the situation of women in her century, that
"The Yellow Wallpaper" emerged five years later.
Witness to the personal and social anguish of its
author, the story is also an indictment of the
incompetent medical advice she received. Charlotte
Perkins Stetson was sent to the most preeminent
"nerve specialist" of her time, Dr. S. Weir Mitchell
of Philadelphia, and it was his patronizing
treatment of her that seems ultimately to have

provoked her to write her story. Dr. Mitchell could not fit Mrs. Stetson into either of his two categories of victims of what was then called "nervous prostration": businessmen exhausted from too much work or society women exhausted from too much play. His prescription for her health was that she devote herself to domestic work and to her child, confine herself to, at most, two hours of intellectual work a day, and "never touch pen, brush or pencil as long as you live."[15]

After a month in Dr. Mitchell's sanitarium Charlotte Stetson returned home. She reports that she almost lost her mind. Like the heroine in her story, she would often "crawl into remote closets and under beds—to hide from the grinding pressure of that profound distress."[16]

In 1887, after four years of marriage, Charlotte Perkins Stetson and her husband agreed to a separation and a divorce. It was an obvious necessity. When away from him—she had made a trip to California shortly after the onset of her illness—she felt healthy and recovered. When she returned to her family she began again to experience depression and fatigue.

For the rest of her life Charlotte Perkins would suffer from the effects of this nervous breakdown. Her autobiography reveals her as a woman of iron will, but also as one who was constantly troubled by periods of severe fatigue and lethargy, against which she fought constantly. Her formidable output of writing, traveling, and lecturing, in the years after her first marriage, would seem to have been wrested from a slim budget of energy, but energy so carefully hoarded and directed that it sustained her through over thirty years as a leading feminist writer and lecturer.

In 1890 Charlotte Perkins Stetson moved to California, where, struggling for economic survival as a woman alone, she began lecturing on the status of women. The years between 1890 and 1894 were, she recalls, the hardest of her life. She was fighting against public opinion, against outright hostility, as she gave her lectures on socialism and freedom for women. She taught school, kept a boarding house, edited newspapers, all the time writing and speaking. She accepted her husband's new marriage to her best friend, to whom she relinquished her child, and this action led to even greater public hostility, of course, against which she had to fight. In the midst of this most difficult period in her life she produced "The Yellow Wallpaper."

The story is narrated with clinical precision and aesthetic tact. The curt, chopped sentences, the brevity of the paragraphs, which often consist of only one or two sentences, convey the taut, distraught mental state of the narrator. The style creates a controlled tension: everything is low key and understated. The stance of the narrator is all, and it is a very complex stance indeed, since she is ultimately mad and yet, throughout her descent into madness, in many ways more sensible than the people who surround and cripple her. As she tells her story the reader has confidence in the reasonableness of her arguments and explanations.

The narrator is a woman who has been taken to the country by her husband in an effort to cure her of some undefined illness—a kind of nervous fatigue. Although her husband, a doctor, is presented as kindly and well meaning, it is soon apparent that his treatment of his wife, guided as it is by nineteenth-century attitudes toward women is an important source of her affliction and a perhaps inadvertent but nonetheless vicious abettor of it. Here is a woman who, as she tries to explain to anyone who will listen, wants very much to *work*. Specifically, she wants to write (and the story she is narrating is her desperate and secret attempt both to engage in work that is meaningful to her and to retain her sanity). But the medical advice she receives, from her doctor/husband, from her brother, also a doctor, and from S. Weir Mitchell, explicitly referred to in the story, is that she do nothing. The prescribed cure is total rest and total emptiness of mind. While she craves intellectual stimulation and activity, and at one point poignantly expresses her wish for "advice and companionship" (one can read today respect and equality) in her work, what she receives is the standard treatment meted out to women in a patriarchal society. Thus her husband sees her as a "blessed little goose."[17] She is his "little girl" and she must take care of herself for his sake. Her role is to be "a rest and comfort to him." That he often laughs at her is, she notes forlornly and almost casually at one point, only what one expects in marriage.

Despite her pleas he will not take her away from this house in the country which she hates. What he does, in fact, is choose for her a room in the house that was formerly a nursery. It is a room with barred windows originally intended to prevent small children from falling out. It is the room with the fateful yellow wallpaper. The narrator herself had preferred a room downstairs; but this is 1890 and, to use Virginia Woolf's phrase, there is no choice for this wife of "a room of one's own."

Without such choice, however, the woman has been emotionally and intellectually violated. In fact, her husband instills guilt in her. They have come to the country, he says "solely on [her] account." Yet this means that he must be away all day, and many nights, dealing with his patients.

The result in the woman is subterfuge. With her husband she cannot be her true self but must pose; and this, as she says, "makes me very tired." Finally, the fatigue and the subterfuge are unbearable. Increasingly she concentrates her attention on the wallpaper in her room—a paper of a sickly yellow that both disgusts and fascinates her. Gilman works out the symbolism of the wallpaper beautifully, without ostentation. For, despite all the elaborate descriptive detail devoted to it, the wallpaper remains mysteriously, hauntingly undefined and only vaguely visuable. But such, of course, is the situation of this wife, who identifies herself with the paper. The paper symbolizes her situation as seen by the men who control her and hence her situation as seen by herself. How can she define herself?

The wallpaper consists of "lame uncertain curves" that suddenly "commit suicide—destroy themselves in unheard-of contradictions." There are pointless patterns in the paper, which the narrator nevertheless determines to pursue to some conclusion. Fighting for her identity, for some sense of independent self, she observes the

Afterword 51

wallpaper and notes that just as she is about to find some pattern and meaning in it, it "slaps you in the face, knocks you down, and tramples upon you."

Inevitably, therefore, the narrator, imprisoned within the room, thinks she discerns the figure of a woman behind the paper. The paper is barred—that is part of what pattern it has, and the woman is trapped behind the bars, trying to get free. Ultimately, in the narrator's distraught state, there are a great many women behind the patterned bars, all trying to get free.

Given the morbid social situation that by now the wallpaper has come to symbolize, it is no wonder that the narrator begins to see it as staining everything it touches. The sickly yellow color runs off, she imagines, on her husband's clothes as well as on her own.

But this woman, whom we have come to know so intimately in the course of her narrative, and to admire for her heroic efforts to retain her sanity despite all opposition, never does get free. Her insights, and her desperate attempts to define and thus cure herself by tracing the bewildering pattern of the wallpaper and deciphering its meaning, are poor weapons against the male certainty of her husband, whose attitude toward her is that "bless her little heart" he will *allow* her to be "as sick as she pleases."

It is no surprise to find, therefore, that at the end of the story the narrator both does and does not identify with the creeping women who surround her in her hallucinations. The women creep out of the wallpaper, they creep through the arbors and lanes and along the roads outside the house. Women must creep. The narrator knows this. She has fought as best she could against creeping. In her perceptivity and in her resistance lie her heroism (her heroineism). But at the end of the story, on her last day in the house, as she peels off yards and yards of wallpaper and creeps around the floor, she has been defeated. She is totally mad.

But in her mad-sane way she has seen the situation of women for what it is. She has wanted to strangle the woman behind the paper—tie her with a rope. For that woman, the tragic product of her society, is of course the narrator's self. By rejecting that woman she might free the other, imprisoned woman within herself. But the only available rejection is suicidal, and hence she descends into madness. Madness is her only freedom, as, crawling around the room, she screams at her husband that she has finally "got out"—outside the wallpaper—and can't be put back. [18]

Earlier in the story the heroine gnawed with her

teeth at the nailed-down bed in her room: excruciating proof of her sense of imprisonment. Woman as prisoner; woman as child or cripple; woman, even, as a fungus growth, when at one point in her narrative the heroine describes the women whom she envisions behind the wallpaper as "strangled heads and bulbous eyes and waddling fungus growths." These images permeate Gilman's story. If they are the images men had of women, and hence that women had of themselves, it is not surprising that madness and suicide bulk large in the work of late nineteenth-century women writers. "Much madness is divinest sense . . . Much sense the starkest madness," Emily Dickinson had written some decades earlier; and she had chosen spinsterhood as one way of rejecting society's "requirements" regarding woman's role as wife. One thinks, too, of Edith Wharton's *The House of Mirth*, with its heroine, Lily Bart, "manacled" by the bracelets she wears. Raised as a decorative item, with no skills or training, Lily must find a husband, if she is to have any economic security. Her bracelets, intended to entice young bachelors, are really her chains. Lily struggles against her fate, trying to retain her independence and her moral integrity. In the end, however, she commits suicide.

Such suicides as that of Lily, or of Kate

Chopin's heroine mentioned earlier, as well as the madness that descends upon the heroine in "The Yellow Wallpaper," are all deliberate dramatic indictments, by women writers, of the crippling social pressures imposed on women in the nineteenth century and the sufferings they thereby endured: women who could not attend college although their brothers could; women expected to devote themselves, their lives, to aging and ailing parents; women treated as toys or as children and experiencing who is to say how much loss of self-confidence as a result. It is to this entire class of defeated, or even destroyed women, to this large body of wasted, or semi-wasted talent, that "The Yellow Wallpaper" is addressed.

The heroine in "The Yellow Wallpaper" is destroyed. She has fought her best against husband, brother, doctor, and even against women friends (her husband's sister, for example, is "a perfect and enthusiastic housekeeper, and hopes for no better profession"). She has tried, in defiance of all the social and medical codes of her time, to retain her sanity and her individuality. But the odds are against her and she fails.

Charlotte Perkins Stetson Gilman did not fail. She had been blighted, damaged, like the heroine in her story, by society's attitudes toward women. But having written the story she transcended the heroine's fate—although at what inner cost we shall never know. She went on to carve out a famous career as a feminist lecturer and writer. From the 1890s until about 1920 she was in demand as a speaker both in the United States and abroad, and her books were read on both continents. The books, especially *Women and Economics*, attacked the social and economic system that enslaved and humiliated women. About this enslavement and humiliation she was adamant, as some of her more striking metaphors show:

That women are kept, like horses:

> The labor of women in the house, certainly, enables men to produce more wealth than they otherwise could; and in this way women are economic factors in society. But so are horses. The labor of horses enables men to produce more wealth than they otherwise could. The horse is an economic factor in society. But the horse is not economically independent, nor is the woman.[19]

That women are used like cows:

The wild cow is a female. She has healthy calves, and milk enough for them. And that is all the femininity she needs. Otherwise than that she is bovine rather than feminine. She is a light, strong, swift, sinewy creature, able to run, jump, and fight, if necessary. We, for economic uses, have artificially developed the cow's capacity for producing milk. She has become a walking milk-machine, bred and tended to that express end, her value measured in quarts. [20]

Women's ineffectual domestic status was the target of some of Gilman's strongest attacks. As she said elsewhere in *Women and Economics*, the same world exists for women as for men,

the same human energies and human desires and ambitions within. But all that she may wish to have, all that she may wish to do, must come through a single channel and a single choice. Wealth, power, social distinction, fame,—not only these, but home and happiness, reputation, ease and pleasure, her bread and butter,—all, must come to her through a small gold ring. [21]

The damaging effects on women of being

manacled to that small gold ring she explored in detail. Women are bred for marriage, yet they cannot actively pursue it but must sit passively and wait to be chosen. The result is strain and hypocrisy, and an overemphasis on sex or "femininity." "For, in her position of economic dependence in the sex-relation, sex-distinction is with her not only a means of attracting a mate, as with all creatures, but a means of getting her livelihood, as is the case with no other creature under heaven." [22]

Gilman was not opposed to the home nor to domestic work. She believed indeed that the home tended to produce such qualities, necessary for the development of the human race, as kindness and caring. But her evolutionary approach to social change enabled her to see that the institution of the home had not developed consonant to the development of other institutions in society. Women, and children, were imprisoned within individual homes, where the women had no recognized economic independence and the children often suffocated, "noticed, studied, commented on, and incessantly interfered with. . . . How can they grow up without injury? [23] For, she argued, in the home as presently established there can be neither freedom nor equality. Rather, there is "ownership": a dominant father, a more or less subservient mother, and an utterly dependent child. Injustice, rather than justice, was the result.

In her attack on the nuclear family Gilman thus anticipated many current complaints. Or, one should rather say, that more than half a century after she began her campaign against women's subservient status we are still struggling with the problems she diagnosed and described.

Her suggested solutions included community kitchens, whereby the work of cooking would be more efficiently and sociably performed, leaving those women free for other occupations who were not adept at this particular skill but meanwhile making that skill economically respectable; and childcare centers—even if only play space on walled-in roofs of city apartment buildings—to release the child and the mother from the tyranny of the individual family.

Work must be respected: this was one of Gilman's basic tenets. but women must be admitted into the human work world on equal terms with men. The domestic work they do must be respected, and they must be free to do other kinds of work as well. Gilman believed in continuing human progress (she wrote a utopian novel, *Moving the Mountain*, in which women had achieved true equality with men), and she saw the situation of women in the nineteenth century as thwarting this progress as well as thwarting their own development. For some human beings to be classified as horses, or cows, or sexual objects, was to impoverish not only themselves but human society as a whole.

She herself refused to be so thwarted. In 1900 she married her cousin, George Houghton Gilman and she continued to work until the day when she chose her own death. Suffering from breast cancer, she chose not to be a burden to others. She took chloroform and died. It was her final willed choice.

Notes

1. William Dean Howells, ed., *The Great Modern American Stories* (New York: Boni and Liveright, 1920), p. vii.

2. Carl Degler, ed., *Women and Economics* (reprint ed., New York: Harper and Row, 1966), p. xiii.

3. Leslie Y. Rabkin, ed., *Psychopathology and*

Literature (San Francisco: Chandler Publications, 1966); Elaine Gottlieb Hemley and Jack Matthews, eds., *The Writer's Signature: Idea in Story and Essay* (Glenview, Ill.: Scott, Foresman, Co., 1972); Gail Parker, ed., *The Oven Brids: American Women on Womanhood, 1820-1920* (Garden City. N.Y.: Anchor Books, 1972). The last of these anthologies is the only one that puts "The Yellow Wallpaper" into the context of the struggle of American women for self-, social, and political expression. However, Dr. Parker's treatment of Gilman in her introduction is negative and sometimes factually shaky. Nor does she discuss the story itself in any detail.

4. Charlotte Perkins Gilman, *The Living of Charlotte Perkins Gilman. An Autobiography* (New York: D. Appleton-Century Co., 1935), p. 119.

5. Ibid., p. 120. It is interesting to note that the writer of this letter, a doctor, ascribed the heroine's problem to "an *heredity* of mental derangement." (My italics.)

6. Ibid., p. 120.

7. Ibid., p. 5. "Whether the doctor's dictum was the reason [for the father's abandoning the family]

or merely a reason I do not know," Gilman writes in her autobiography.

8. Ibid., p. 44.

9. Ibid.

10. Ibid., p. 45.

11. Ibid., p. 61.

12. Ibid., pp. 82, 83.

13. Ibid., p. 83 (My italics.)

14. Ibid., pp. 83, 87-8, 89, 91

15. Ibid., p. 96

16. Ibid.

17. "The Yellow Wall-Paper," *The New England Magazine*, May 1892, p. 649. (Since the reader has the text in this present edition, subsequent page references to the original printing seem unnecessary).

18. At this point, at the end of her story, Gilman

has the narrator say to her husband, "I've got out at last, . . . in spite of you and Jane." There has been no previous reference to a "Jane" in the story, and so one must speculate as to the reference. It could conceivably be a printer's error, since there are both a Julia and a Jennie in the story (Jennie is the housekeeper and functions as a guardian/imprisoner for the heroine, and Julia is an ineffectual female relative). On the other hand, it could be that Gilman is referring here to the narrator herself, to the narrator's sense that she has gotten free of both her husband and her "Jane" self: free, that is, of herself as defined by marriage and society.

19. *Women and Economics*, p. 13.

20. Ibid., pp. 43-44.

21. Ibid., p. 71.

22. Ibid., p. 38.

23. *The Home: Its Work and Influence* (New York: Charlton Co., 1910), pp. 40-41.

For a free, complete backlist catalog, write to The Feminist Press at The City University of New York, 311 East 94 Street, New York, NY 10128. Send book orders to The Talman Company, Inc., 150 Fifth Avenue, New York, NY 10011. Please include $1.75 for postage and handling for one book, $.75 for each additional.